Grandma's Lap

Regina C. Moore

J. Kenkade
PUBLISHING

Bryant, Arkansas

J. Kenkade Publishing

5920 Highway 5 N. Ste. 7

Bryant, AR 72022

Social Media: @jkenkadepublishing

www.jkenkadepublishing.com

J. Kenkade Publishing is a national
midsize publisher.
The J. Kenkade Publishing name and logo
are registered trademarks.

Printed in the United States of America.

ISBN 978-1-955186-34-6

This book is dedicated to grandmothers everywhere! To my Madea, Matilda Smith, and my grandmamma Roxie. To my mother, Minnie B. Cloman, my church family, my children and grandchildren—especially the daughters of the Smith family.
To my Heavenly Father, I owe you everything.
Thank you for the gift of writing!

It was a cold and bright December morning. The sun was up, and I was in a hurry to start my day. Mom and Dad were already up. They had been preparing for this trip for a long time. You see, this was an important day, a very special day for the Smith family.

Anyone not ready when Dad gave the final "All Aboard!" was left behind. The baby was still asleep in her crib, unaware of the events that lay ahead: the same events that awaited me twelve years ago, our mother forty years before, and her mother before her.

Today, the tradition continues—a tradition that has determined the fate and outcome of each of our families. For nearly one hundred years, every baby girl born to the Smith family has been taken many, many miles outside of town, down past the Old Mill, through Sunset Grove to a place few people travel, to a little house that sits alone, as if time stands still, to be blessed on Grandma's Lap.

It is a quiet little home. It has no electricity. The wood stove is still in use, the trees are still green, and the flowers are still in bloom. Everything is picture perfect, if you ask me. Yet, there is one thing that makes Grandma's house more special than any other in the whole world…

Surrounding her home, as it has for nearly one hundred years stood a rainbow, beautifully arrayed with colors as bright as the sun.

For years, many have tried to explain its existence, but to no avail. Grandma never offered any tall tales about her rainbow.

"Just showed up," she'd say.
"The source of her powers," others would say.
"The good Lord put it here. He'll take it in His own good time," said grandma.

All of the neighbors are gone now. Only she remains. A passerby or two would, every now and then, show up in hopes of getting a glimpse of her or the rainbow.

"Only the pure in heart can see my bow," Grandma would say.

Of course, all of the women in the Smith family can see it too.

Matilda is her name but some call her Roxie. To us, she is simply Madea. She's one hundred and twenty years old and counting. No one knows how or why she has survived so long. Most swear it's the power of the *Bow*. Grandma offered no tall tales.

> *"The good Lord's lettin' me stay here. He'll take me when He's good and ready."*

Grandma was a praying woman. If you were in need of a miracle, she was the one to call. Long ago, as the story is told, Minnie, Grandma's sister, gave birth to a beautiful baby girl.

One very cold and bright December morning, the baby became ill and almost died. Minnie was very upset and didn't know what to do. As she sat in her house and prayed, she heard a voice that sweetly whispered, *"Matilda's lap."*

Minnie thought she was hearing things until she
heard the voice whisper again, *"Matilda's lap."* Minnie
didn't hesitate. She wrapped her baby in a blanket and
began her journey. She knew that the journey could
very well be the end of her and her darling baby girl.

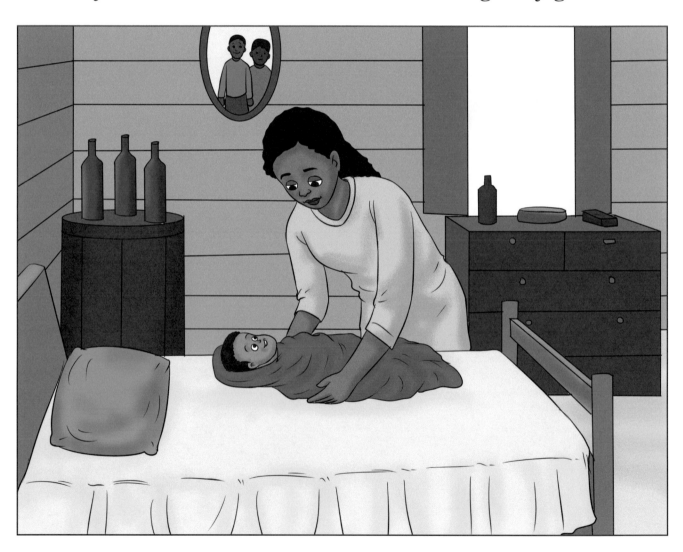

She walked for miles and miles. The roads were covered with ice and snow, but Minnie was determined to keep going. She knew she had to hurry or her precious baby would die!

When she finally arrived, Grandma was standing on the porch. She looked at Minnie and said, "I've been waiting for you."

They rushed into the house! Grandma sat down, and Minnie placed the baby on her lap. Grandma quickly wrapped the baby girl in her favorite blanket. It was the very same blanket her grandma wrapped her in when she was a baby.

The fabric was worn and its color was now fading, yet each piece tells a story of our family from long ago. It was stitched in love and sewn in grace; now it holds a power that can never be erased.

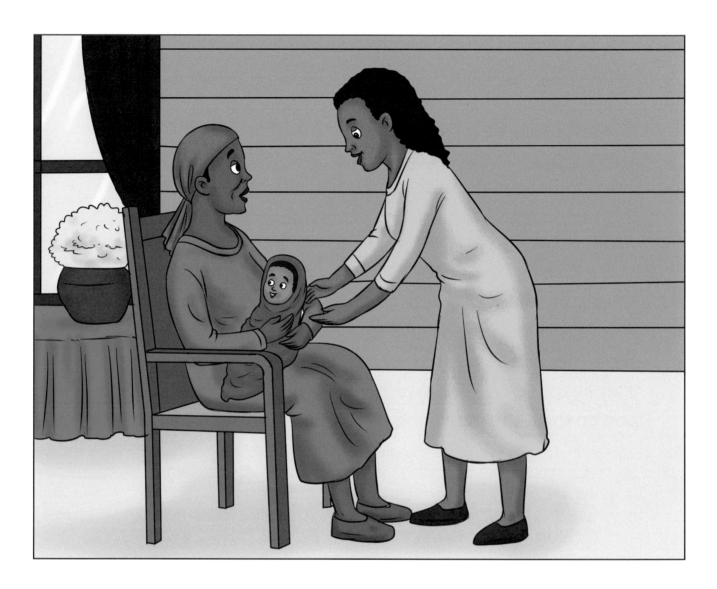

Grandma held the baby close to her heart. She lay very still as if no life remained, until Grandma spoke these words...

"Arise, sweet baby. No more sickness—no more. The glory of my Lord is with you. He's standing at the door. Arise, sweet baby. No more sickness—no more! You are resting on Grandma's Lap. Arise and soar!"

Right then and there, the baby's eyes opened, and the sickness was gone! It was a miracle! A miracle that no one could explain. But Grandma knew. She knew God, and she knew He was a healer.

The baby was sleeping peacefully as Grandma took her while still wrapped in her blanket, and laid her on the bed.

From that moment, she was never sick another day in her life. Nor were her children or her children's children.

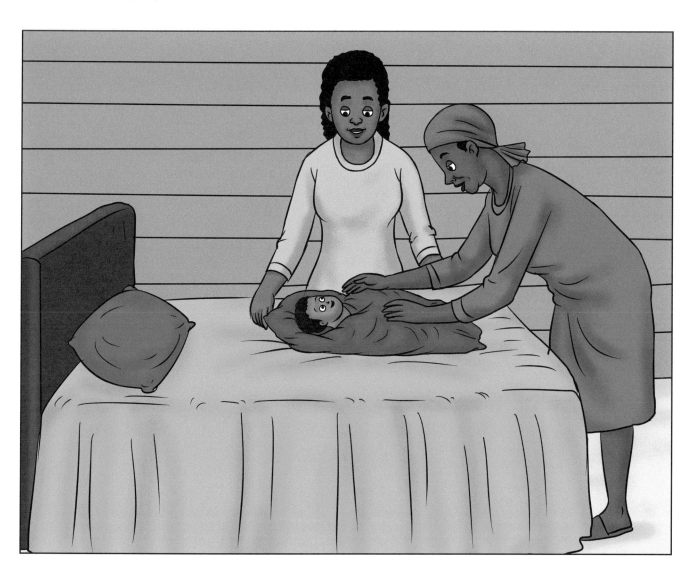

Our tradition began on that special day. That is the day the rainbow came, and ever since that day, every baby girl born to the Smith family is taken many, many miles outside of town, down past the Old Mill, through Sunset Grove...

to a place few people travel, to a little house that sits alone as if time stands still.

It is a place of joy and harmony, a place where God abides to bless the Smith daughters...

on Grandma's lap.

The End.

Made in the USA
Columbia, SC
09 February 2025

52959564R00018